Toby, The Turtle Who Could Sing

by
Emily
C.
Harrison

Illustrations by Bruce Andrews
Emily Hill, Editor

Pp
Patches Publishing
Montevallo Alabama

ISBN 0-9666814-0-1

Published by: Patches Publishing
230 Country Ridge Road
Montevallo, Alabama 35115
Additional copies or original artwork
may be purchased from the publisher.

Printed by: Image Graphics, Paducah, KY
Print/Publishing/Design Consultants:
Douglas Eason and Billy Blackman, Havana, FL

Dedication

To Dr. Norman Johnson,
my high school choral director
at Thompson High School—

Thanks for inspiring me to "keep on singing."

Toby, The Turtle
Who Could Sing

One rainy day
Toby, the turtle,
was sitting on
a riverbank by himself.
He was not an
ordinary turtle.

He could do something no other turtle could do—
He could sing.
Oh, how he could sing!

He sang in any kind of weather . . .
rainy weather, sunny weather,
or frosty weather.

Toby would sing all the time
in his beautiful, charming voice.
But he did not have any friends.
The other animals thought he was strange
because he could sing.

So Toby became lonely
for a long, long time.
After four sad years of being by himself,
something wonderful finally happened to Toby—

One morning when he
was hiding in his shell
close to the pond,
Toby suddenly heard a lovely voice
coming from above.
He quickly popped his head out of his shell
and glanced up.

He saw Sunshine, a beautiful canary with soft feathers of
pale yellow, resting on a tree limb above him.
Her voice was like a wind chime carrying a
peaceful melody through the air.

When Toby started to ask Sunshine
why she was singing to *him*, they
both noticed Ivory, an elegant
swan, swimming in the water.

"You have the most beautiful voice
I have ever heard," Ivory said to Sunshine.
"Why is it so cheerful?"
Sunshine replied, "It is cheerful because
I like to make everyone joyful."

Toby overheard Sunshine talking to Ivory,
and he began to sing.
Ivory, overcome with envy, said to Toby,
"You can sing, too?"

Toby nodded and answered,
"If you believe in yourself, you can do anything you want to do.
You can make all your dreams come true."

Ivory said sadly, "I cannot sing.
I can only dance."
"That's excellent!" responded Toby.
"I wish I could dance!"

Toby then saw a brilliant glow
appear in Ivory's eyes,
and this delighted him.

So with the help of Sunshine,
Toby began to sing once more.

And Ivory began to dance.
She danced and fluttered her graceful wings
upon the sparkling pond
to the sound of their music.

The other animals from the forest heard the
lively music and gathered to watch and listen.

After the music ended, the animals were so pleased
with what they had seen and heard, they built a
stage of wood and straw for Toby,
Sunshine, and Ivory.

Toby was happy once again
because of his new friends,
and because he could do the thing he liked
to do most in life . . .
and that was to sing
and make everyone happy.

And he did . . .
having many more
exciting adventures
along the way.